Woo hoo! The book version of *Dr. Slump* is out! Yaaay! It's been a long time coming, and it's thanks to you fans! Yaaay! At last, Arale gets to say "N'cha!" in the book! Thanks for reading, good little boys and girls. Now, go have fun in Penguin Village!

—Akira Toriyama, 1980

鳥山 明

DR. SLUMP VOL. 1
The SHONEN JUMP Graphic Novel Edition

STORY AND ART BY
AKIRA TORIYAMA

English Adaptation & Translation/Alexander O. Smith
Touch-up Art & Lettering/Walden Wong
Design/Sean Lee
Editor/Yuki Takagaki

Managing Editor/Elizabeth Kawasaki
Director of Production/Noboru Watanabe
Vice President of Publishing/Alvin Lu
Vice President & Editor in Chief/Yumi Hoashi
Sr. Director of Acquisitions/Rika Inouye
Vice President of Sales & Marketing/Liza Coppola
Publisher/Hyoe Narita

Printed in the U.S.A.

Published by VIZ, LLC
P.O. Box 77010
San Francisco, CA 94107

10 9 8 7 6 5 4 3 2 1
First printing, April 2005

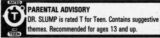

THE WORLD'S
MOST POPULAR MANGA

SHONEN
JUMP
GRAPHIC NOVEL
www.shonenjump.com

www.viz.com

SHONEN JUMP GRAPHIC NOVEL

Story & Art by
Akira Toriyama

Table of Contents!

DR. SLUMP
Vol. 1

The Birth of Arale!

*NORIMAKI SENBEI: A RICE CRACKER WRAPPED IN SEAWEED

ZZZZZT

ZZZZZT

SNUFFLE, SNUFFLE ...

YAWN.

WHEW ...

HMM. SHOULD'VE PUT THE TALKING BITS ON LAST.

BO-RING.

ALLEY-OOP!

OKAY.

THERE! TRY WIGGLING YOUR ARM.

BUG EYES.

WIGGLE! JUST WIGGLE!

WHA... WHA...

SILENCE!

MY CHEST'S ALL FLAT.

THOUGHT I WAS A GONER...

7

8

NO.

HOW ABOUT A TUMMY MISSILE? *BAZOOOM!*

WHO SAID ANYTHING ABOUT FIGHTING EVIL!?

THEN WHAT WILL I USE TO FIGHT THE FORCES OF EVIL?

FEMININE CHARM ...?

HUH?

ARE MY EYES BAD?

WHAT NOW?

HEY.

GAH! THIS WON'T DO!

DOCTOR, YOUR FACE LOOKS ALL GOOFY.

HOW ABOUT THIS?

WHAT!?

N

READ THIS.

S

T

ER... THIS ONE?

TOTALLY OFF...

U

?

ARE YOU MAKING FUN OF ME!?

SILENCE!

WOW! KING KONG!

WOW! EVERY-THING'S SO CLEAR!

10

WAIT HERE. I'LL GO BUY YOU SOME CLOTHES.

GOING OUT, DOCTOR?

CAN'T HAVE YOU WEARING MY PJs FOREVER.

WHO TAUGHT YOU THAT?

A MINK COAT?

LET'S SEE... GOT THAT, THAT...

WHAT'S LEFT?

THE STORE

50% OFF SALE

THE STORE

EVERYTHING HALF OFF

DIAPERS & MISSILES IN STOCK!!

UNDER-WEAR.

A-HA! I KNOW!

BLAST! THEY'LL THINK I'M A PERVERT FOR SURE!

LOOK, IT'S NOT FOR ME! IT'S A PRESENT FOR MY MOTHER!

I HAVE A DRESS THAT WOULD LOOK SPLENDID ON YOU, SIR.

HEH HEH. FOR THE MISSUS, YOU KNOW.

...AND LIPSTICK?

SWOOSH

THANK YOU! COME AGAIN!

AH! I KNOW JUST THE THING.

POP

SKRIK SKRIK

TOILET

WELCOME!

▪ = WOMEN ▪ = MEN

BLAST! THIS IS PATHETIC!

SQUEAK SQUEAK

MMMPH

FORGET IT, BUDDY. YOU AIN'T MY TYPE.

WHO GIVES THEIR MOTHER A SCHOOL-GIRL UNIFORM!?

IDIOT STORE CLERK!

THESE, PERHAPS?

ER... MA'AM...?

UH...

UM...ER... P-PANTIES, PLEASE. PANTIES.

SQUIRM

SQUIRM...

OH DEAR, TERRIBLY SORRY! OH!

OH! OH-HO!

THEY'RE NOT FOR ME!!

I LOOK LIKE A BOY.

...THE MOST EMBARRASSING DAY OF MY LIFE.

5 O'CLOCK SHADOW

14

IF NO ONE NOTICES YOU'RE A ROBOT, I WIN!

SIR!

OKAY, LET'S TRY GOING OUTSIDE!

BOING BOING

STOP THAT!!

N' CHA!*

*SENBEI'S GREETING

COFFEE Pot

DOCTOR WHAT!?

OH, DOCTOR SKUNK!

NONSENSE! I'M ONLY 28! SHE'S...MY SISTER!

YOUR DAUGHTER, SENBEI?

N'CHA!

HEY.

WHAT'S YOUR NAME?

YOU DON'T LOOK ALIKE AT ALL! GOOD FOR YOU, SWEETIE.

...

JUST BACK OFF!

WHAT FUNNY NAMES YOU BOTH HAVE!

WHAT HE SAYS!

WHAT'S MY NAME?

URK! YOUR NAME-- RIGHT! UM... ARALE! ARALE NORIMAKI!*

*ARALE: A SMALL RICE CRACKER

16

WHAT?

ENGINE OIL.

WHAT WOULD YOU LIKE, ARALE?

COFFEE FOR ME, THANKS.

WON'T I RUST?

WHEW.

J-JUICE! SHE'LL HAVE JUICE!

YOU DON'T *LOOK* LIKE YOU'RE IN JUNIOR HIGH.

I'M STILL BRAND NEW!

SAY, HOW OLD ARE YOU?

HA HA, GOOD ONE! THIRTEEN! YOU'RE THIRTEEN!

17

YOU DON'T MIND, DO YA?

NOPE!

WHY NOT?

NO MORE QUESTIONS!

S-SOMETHING WRONG WITH HER NOSE?

ZOIK

SAY, YOUR NOSE...

?

NEITHER DO I! THIS IS A MANGA FOR CRYING OUT LOUD! A MANGA!

THUD

YOU DON'T HAVE NOSTRILS!

HEY, YOU'RE RIGHT! NO RUNNY NOSES!

18

GOOD-BYE! GOOD-BYE! GOOD BYE-BYE!

OKAY, THIS IS GETTING SILLY. LET'S GO HOME.

SCREEEECH
KIIIIN
WHAM
BOING

THAT... THAT LITTLE GIRL KNOCKED OVER THE CAR!

...

WOBBLE WOBBLE...

OOPS. MY SHIRT RIPPED.

19

FREEBIE

FUN CARD

You can cut it out and put it in your wallet, fold it into a paper airplane, or crumple it up and trash it! Fun!

If you really cut this out, it'll mess up the comic on the other side...but if you must cut it out, how about buying another copy? No, that's a waste of paper... Just photocopy it.

Dr. SLUMP

ARALE

Arale Norimaki

Here Comes Arale!

...

MORNING, DOCTOR! TIME TO WAKE UP!

DOCTOR!

POP

SNAP

THUNK

GOOD MORNING!

WABOOM

22

MAN! I HAD THE *SCARIEST* DREAM.

SCHOOL STARTS TODAY, RIGHT?

HMM? OH, RIGHT...

DON'T DO ANYTHING ROBOT-LIKE, GOT IT?

YES, SIR!

ZZZIMMM

THAT'S WHAT I MEAN! STOP THAT!

23

PENGUIN VILLAGE MIDDLE SCHOOL

WELL, WELL. IF IT ISN'T DOCTOR NORIMAKI...

YO!

HA HA HA HA HA HA HA HA HA HA HA HA HA HA HA...

STILL, I'M SURPRISED. I DIDN'T KNOW YOU HAD SUCH A YOUNG SISTER.

YOU WERE SICK IN THE HOSPITAL ALL THAT TIME? POOR THING!

SHE'S MY DAUGHTER!

PSST! ACTUALLY...

OH!?

WEREN'T YOU QUITE YOUNG WHEN YOUR PARENTS PASSED AWAY?

BUT WAIT...

GAH

AH, THIS IS YOUR TEACHER, MS. YAMABUKI!

EXCUSE ME...

RATTLE

KRRRRICK

HER BROTHER SENBEI.

NICE... TO MEET YOU.

YES, AND THIS IS HER FATHER, DOCTOR--

YUP.

SO, YOU'RE MISS NORIMAKI?

WELL, CLASS WILL BE STARTING SOON.

BYE'CHA!

OH! RIGHT... SEE YOU LATER, THEN!

I WAS JOKING!

B-BUT YOU JUST SAID...!

YOU'RE A RARE BREED-- A TRUE PERVERT...

WHOO... PRETTY LADY.

WHEW

BAM

25

OH!

I HOPE ARALE'S GOING TO BE OKAY IN THERE.

GIVE ME A RIDE INTO TOWN, SENBEI! IT'S MATINEE DAY!

HUH? OH, IT'S YOU.

HEY! GREAT TIMING!

EVERYONE, PLEASE WELCOME ARALE NORIMAKI.

7th Grade

SHE'LL BE IN THIS CLASS STARTING TODAY.

IN RETURN, YOU CAN BUY ME A TICKET.

LET ME OUT.

YOU WANT OUT? BE MY GUEST!

VROOOOM

PHOOOO

...

HI! NICE TO MEET YOU.

MMRF MMRF

WHAAACHOO

KOOCHY-KOO.

...

WHAT'S YOUR NAME?

WHAT'S YOUR PROBLEM!?

HEE HEE

NO ONE SAID YOU HAD TO COME!

- Adults   1300
- Students 1100
- Children   800
- Infants   200

YOU'RE NOT SEEING THIS... ARE YOU?

Nekotoraman vs. Nekotora-7

HEY!

Nekotoraman vs. Nekotora-7

● Double Feature with Muscleman vs. Heidi of the Alps

HEEE

28

WHAT'S WITH HER?

...

HUH?

JUST LET GO, OKAY?

WHY'S SHE FOLLOWING ME!?

SHE'S THE NEW SUPER KID.

HUH?

HEH HEH... SHE SAYS YOU'RE FRIENDS!

SAYS WHO!?

'CAUSE WE'RE FRIENDS!

YEAH, WHY?

BAD!

DON'T HANG WITH US. WE'RE BAD, 'KAY?

31

I TOLD YOU TO STOP WEARING THAT STUFF!!

TARO!?

CUTE!

PLUB PLUB

HEH. YOU GOT GUTS, KIDDO.

IS SHE MAKING FUN OF YOU?

OR THIS IS YOUR FACE!! THAT ONLY HURT A LITTLE.

I LOVE HOW HE MAKES STUPID STUFF LOOK SO COOL.

GRRRR

BUT YOU BETTER WATCH IT!

CRUNCH

35

Gatchan

Senbei Norimaki

Something's Missing!

THE DOCTOR'S WORST
NIGHTMARE COMES TRUE...
ARALE IS INCOMPLETE!

BUT DOCTOR,
I THOUGHT I
WAS THE PERFECT
HUMANOID
ROBOT...

MY GENIUS...
HAS FAILED!?

ARALE IS MISSING
HER [*CENSORED*]...?

EVERYONE ELSE HAS ONE!

IT'S REAL IMPORTANT.

I DON'T HAVE ONE.

I ...

HUH?

Y-YOU DON'T MEAN...?

S-SOME-THING R-REAL IMPORTANT?

THUMP

WHOA WHOA WHOA !!

MY RE...

SLAP

YEAH.

L-LITTLE KIDS ARE READING THIS!

ARALE, FOR THE LOVE OF...

?

WHEW

HUFF

HUFF

HUFF

YOU DON'T **NEED** ONE!

L-LOOK, TRUST ME.

WHUMP

I WANT ONE, TOO!!

ACK ACK ACK ACK

YOU LIED TO ME.

YOU SAID I WAS THE **PERFECT** HUMANOID ROBOT.

IT...IT WASN'T MY FAULT!

NO... HOW COULD THIS HAVE HAPPENED? MY WORST FEARS...

THERE WAS A REASON!

H-HOW COULD I HAVE KNOWN?

THAT'S IT! A-HA!

I'M A *SCIENTIST*, NOT A PEEPING--

I KNOW, WE COULD PEEK!

CLAP

LEZZGO!

PATTER PATTER

YAAAY! WOO-HOO!

WE'LL GET TO SEE ONE!

I'LL GET TO SEE IT ALL! HEE HEE!

I... I'LL GET TO SEE IT!

HUFF HUFF

SNAP SNAP

I FORGOT!

I'M A GENIUS!

CLICK CLANK

WORK WORK

YOU'RE DOING THIS FOR ME, RIGHT?

O-OF COURSE!!

WHY NOT?

A-ARALE... LISTEN, DON'T DO THAT, OKAY? JUST *DON'T*.

YAY!

I CAN'T WAIT TO SHOW EVERY-BODY!

IT WORKS!

THESE MAKE EVERYTHING INORGANIC TURN TRANSPARENT!

SEE-THRU GLASSES!

WHAT IS IT?

SCARY.

I JUST PUT THESE ON...

ERGO!

...BE-COMES THIS!

AND THIS...

TWIST

THEY CAN WEAR ALL THE CLOTHES THEY WANT--

LOOK! A MOUSE IN THE RAFTERS!

LEMME TRY!

OH, RIGHT. YOU'RE A ROBOT.

HUH !?

44

45

WHOA!

BUS

TH-THUMP
TH-THUMP
THUD
THUD
THUD
THUD
TH-THUMP
TH-THUMP
TH-THUMP
TH-THUMP
THUD
THUD

L-LET'S BEGIN.

BA-BING

BA-BING

SNORT SNORT

THIS IS F-FOR SCIENTIFIC PURPOSES, OKAY?

YOU'RE DROOLING.

L-LOOK... I'M... I'M DOING...

N'CHA!

WAAAH

YO, ARALE!

HEY!

WAH

HUH!?

COVER YOUR- SELF!

WAAAH! WAH! WAH!

YO, DR. N.

THOSE ARE FUNNY- LOOKING SUN- GLASSES.

C-CAN I S-SIT HERE? I PROMISE N-NOT TO DO ANYTHING WEIRD.

S-SURE...

HUH!?

R-RIGHT. I SHOULD JUST GO IN CLOSE. THERE'S NOTHING STOPPING ME...

WHAT'S WITH HIM?

WHAT !?

YEAH, YOUR CAT'S IN THE WAY.

UM...IS SOMETHING THE MATTER?

POKE POKE

!?

OH! N-NOTHING !!

... URF ...

SCRAM! BEAT IT!

PSST!

SNIFF SNIFF

WHAM-O

49

HEY.

G-GIVE THOSE BACK! *NOW!*

AN EENSY-WEENSY BIT.

HUH? SOME-THING'S STICKING OUT?

AAH!

SUPERMAN

AIN'T THAT MS. YAMABUKI?

WHOOSH

WH-WHAT!? MS. *YAMA-BUKI* !?

RIGHT! I HAVE TO SEE FROM THE FRONT!

WHOA! WHOA, WHOA, WHOA !!

WHOOO

SO, DID YOU SEE HER BELLY BUTTON?

HER WH-WHA...?

Akane Kimidori

Taro Soramame

Dr. Monster

ARALE

GODZILLA

Height: 164 feet
Weight: 22,046 tons
• Breathes an atomic ray

GAMERA

Height: 197 feet
Weight: 88 tons
• Breathes fire

SENBEI

Height: 5 feet 7 inches
Weight: 36 pounds
• Drools

54

THAT'LL BE $14, SIR.

LET'S SEE ...

H-HEY, MISTER! HOW MUCH FOR THIS!?

UM, WELL ...

ANYONE EVER TELL YOU YOU LOOK LIKE TOM CRUISE? KNOCK OFF $5, WILL YA?

S-SAY !

PLUB!

FOURTEEN DOLLARS.

SLAM

THE COAST IS CLEAR ...

GOOD, GOOD.

DR. SENBEI NORIMAKI

I NEED CASH. NOW.

SO, AS YOU CAN SEE...

SO, ARALE...

UH-HUH?

WHAT ARE YOU UP TO?

HUH?

CLICK

WHIRR

MAKING A SPARE FACE.

NO JUNIOR HIGH STUDENT LOOKS LIKE THAT!

ARE YOU MAD!?

SO, NO?

WHAT DO YOU THINK?

WELL?

AWW... I LIKED IT.

CLICK CLICK

MAKE YOURSELF USEFUL AND GO BUY ME SOME SMOKES.

N' CHA!

ZOIK

HERE GOES!!

SO FAR, SO GOOD.

WAIT, IT'S JUST A KID...

SCARED THE HEEBIE-JEEBIES OUTTA ME.

G-GAH! WHOO! I'M KINDA LOST, SEE, AND...

HUH?

L-LOOK, COME WITH ME, AND I'LL BUY YOU ANYTHING YA WANT.

ANY-THING?

YES!!

A-HA!

KID NAP

YUP!

SAY, LITTLE GIRL. YOU LIVE HERE?

CRASH

GAMERA!

WHAT'LL IT BE? CHOCOLATE? A LOLLI-POP?

SO!

'C-COURSE I KNOW GAMERA!

GAH

THEY DON'T CALL ME "DR. MONSTER" FOR NOTHING!

YOU DON'T KNOW GAMERA?

W-WHOA! SORRY! YOU OKAY?

THAT WAS THE LAST THING I EXPECTED YA TO SAY...

O-OH, HE'LL GROW QUICK!

HE ALWAYS LOOKED SO BIG.

HUH? WHAT GAME IS THIS?

UH... C-COPS 'N' ROBBERS!

King Ghidra Heights

BE RIGHT BACK!

YUP!

SHH

I'M GOING TO RUN OUT FOR A BIT, SO YOU SIT HERE REAL QUIET LIKE. GOT IT?

WHAT WAS THAT NAME? NORIMAKI...

THE DOCTOR'S CIGA-RETTES!

OH, NO!

N... N-A... N-I... N--

NORI-MAKI... N... N...

TELEPHONE

59

NORIMAKI... NORIMAKI... ARRRGH!

ALLEY-OOP!

TH-THERE! FOUND IT!

HERE, CIGAR-ETTES!

...

THAT TOOK YOU A WHILE.

YES, DR. NORIMAKI SPEAKING.

BRRRRING

AAAH... D-DIS IS DR. MONSTER...

HEY, ARALE. IT'S A "DR. MONSTER" FOR YOU.

H-HELLO? YER WASTIN' YER TIDE! SHE'S... HELLO?

OH, ARALE? YEAH, SHE'S RIGHT HERE, JUST A SEC.

YOU HAB A DAWDER ...?

AAAH !?

&#$% !?

I FORGOT GAMERA! I'LL BE RIGHT THERE!

OH, RIGHT!

WHERE'D SHE GO!?

IF SHE RUNS OUT OF ENERGY, HER COVER WILL BE BLOWN!

ARALE'S ENERGY: ROBOVITA A

ARALE, IT'S ABOUT TIME FOR YOUR RECHARGE ...

A-ARALE !?

HUH !?

I'M GOING HOME NOW.

BYE' CHA! THANKS FOR GAMERA.

H-HOW DID SHE CUT THE ROPES !?

I J-JUST REMEMBERED I GOT AN ERRAND TO RUN!

AAAH !

W-WAIT A SEC!

SO, YOU PROMISE YOU WON'T LEAVE THIS TIME?

YOU THINK YOU COULD WATCH MY PLACE FOR A BIT?

SURE, NO PROBLEM!

THAT'S "ARALE" ...

SNIFF TH-THANKS, AERIAL!

"A-AERIAL" ... WAS IT ?

'KAY?

RIGHT !

...

SLAM

SORRY, AKANE HASN'T SEEN HER, EITHER.

NO.

HMM? ARALE ...?

I'VE DONE IT!

AND IN ONLY ONE FRAME!

K-9 ROBOT

BZZT CLANG
CRASH BZZT CLANG
TAT-TAT-TAT-TAT

WHY AM I SNIFFING A ROBOT'S UNDERWEAR?

SNIFF SNIFF

GO! FIND THE OWNER OF THESE!

64

Dear Dr. Monster,

As a thank-you for Gamera, I'm sending this baby Godzilla I found in the garden. When they get big, let's have them fight!

Arale

67

Which Will It Be?

71

NNG!

NNG!!

KAAANG

KOON...G!!

BRAAP

H-HI! B-BYE!

OOH! LOOK, IT'S TARO!

LESSEE...

WHERE COULD ARALE BE?

SEE?

MR. TARO SORA-MAME!

H-HEY, TEACH.

YOU LOOK GOOD IN SHADES... AND IS THAT A CIGARETTE YOU'VE GOT THERE? A MODEL NINTH GRADER!

DID YOU SEE THAT? CHICKS DIG ME!

SNAP

I KNEW IT! I AM THE MALE HEART-THROB IN THIS MANGA!

72

HEY, THERE SHE IS.

HEH... HEH...

TWITCH TWITCH

H-HEY! HEY, HEY, HEY!

TRACK...?

NOW, ARALE, I THINK YOU'D BE PERFECT FOR TRACK.

ANYWAY, I CALLED HER FIRST!

LIAR! NOT ACCORDING TO HER!

BASE-BALL...?

NOT SO FAST! ARALE'S ON THE BASEBALL TEAM!

THUD

SUMO?

NUH-UH! I CALLED HER WAY BEFORE YOU DID!

WHY DO YOU WANT A GIRL PLAYING BASE-BALL, ANYWAY!?

AH, YES! RATHER, NO! I DON'T SEE!

WELL IT'S KIND OF...SORT OF...MAYBE LIKE...YOU SEE?

HEY HEY HEY

YO YO YO YO

WHAT'S GOING ON HERE, MS. YAMABUKI?

OH, MR. PRINCIPAL.

ARE...ALL THOSE OUR STUDENTS?

WELL...

IT DOES SEEM A BIT MUCH FOR 65 STUDENTS.

I WASN'T AWARE WE HAD SO MANY TEAMS AT OUR SCHOOL.

HEY, AKANE! I DON'T GOTTA PAY, DO I?

T-T-T-TURTLE...

IN LINE, PAL!

SHH! THIS IS MY CAMEO!

HUH? DR. N?

ALL RIGHT, LISTEN UP! AS ARALE'S MANAGER I'LL BE CHARGING A SMALL FEE...

HUH!?

?

I'M OUTTA HERE.

76

LIKE A FROG AWAKENING FROM A LONG WINTER IN THE MUD!

AAAH! I HAVE EMERGED!

IT'S DEEP! REAL DEEP!

I CAN SEE CHINA!

HEY! CAN YOU HEAR ME!?

YOO HOOO!

TITTER TITTER

SNIFF I...I'M T-TELLING MOMMY... SNIFF

He's no wimp, either!

SEE!? AIN'T SHE SOMETHIN'!?

CAN I THROW IT HARD THIS TIME?

DA... DA...

I WANT HER!

GIANTS 90

78

WHOO WHOO

HEY! SHE'S COMING DOWN!

THIS IS TAKING IT A BIT FAR...

EEK!

VRRROOSH!

LI... LI...

ZOOOOP

N'CHA.

PLONK

LITTLE GIRLS! LITTLE GIRLS FROM HEAVEN!

RIGHT! NEXT!

...

WHOA.

CAPTAIN, OUR BALL!

WHAP

AAAH!?

VOLLEYBALL

...

PITTER-PAT-PAT-PAT

RUGBY

HUH? THIS ONE?

BOXING

YEEEAA- AAARGH!

THUUUP

FLOWER ARRANGEMENT!?

82

WHEE
WHEE

GIGGLE
GIGGLE

ARF
ARF

WOOT
WOOT

BAA
BAA

MOO

CAW
CAW

GAAOOW!
(GODZILLA)

PEEP
PEEP

*A TV SHOW ABOUT A GIRL WHO HELPS THE POLICE CATCH CRIMINALS.

Peasuke Soramame

Ms. Midori Yamabuki

Bearly Friends!

HI, ARALE!

OH!

OH, AKANE WAS DRINKING SUPER PUNCH AT LUNCH, AND THE PRINCIPAL GOT MAD AT HER.

THAT WEIRD DRINK!?

N' CHA!

NOT PLAYING WITH AKANE TODAY?

HEY, ARALE !

WANT TO SEE SOMETHING UNUSUAL ?

LIKE A WORM'S PEE-PEE ?

SOME-THING UNUSUAL ...?

A-ARALE !

86

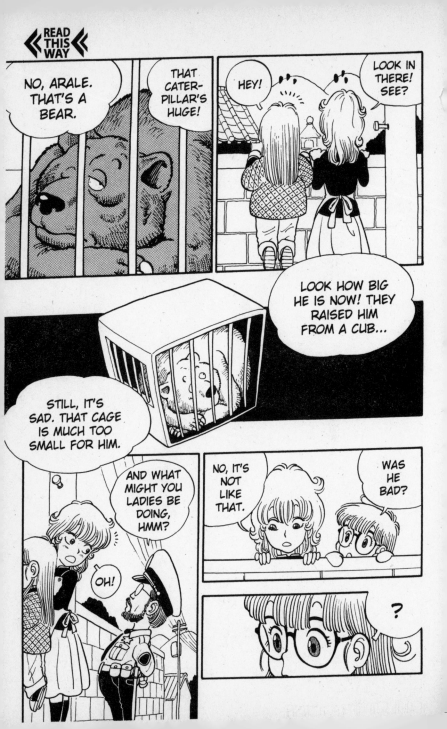

SHE'S GOT DEDICATION, BUT I'M AFRAID SHE LACKS SKILL.

WHAT'S SHE UP TO? SHE RAN IN AND STARTED SEWING...

FINALLY! SHE'S BECOMING LIKE A REAL GIRL! I GET IT!

A STUFFED ANIMAL! WHY, IT'S A MONKEY!

AAAH!

HEH HEH! YOU'LL SOON BE BIG ENOUGH FOR STUFFING!

GRRRRR

RAP RAP RAP

NO FOOD FOR YOU!

F-FOUL BEAST! BACK! BACK!

WHOA!

ROWRRR

88

C'MON!

OOF!

SPROING

!!

THUD BUMP THUMP

UM... HUH?

HEY, ARALE! IT'S THE MIDDLE OF THE NIGHT! KEEP IT--

HYAAARGH!

WHAT THE...!?

EH!?

SWAP

HUH!?

SWAP

BAD MEN GO FLY...*

WAH!

LIKE THIS!

ZOP

HEY, ARALE! HELP ME GET HIM IN THE CAR, QUICK!

WELL, THE HEAD SEEMS INTACT.

...

*"GO FLY" = "GO FLYING." ARALE IS STILL LEARNING TO TALK, AND SHE OCCASIONALLY ABBREVIATES. WE APOLOGIZE FOR ANY INCONVENIENCE.

99

FREEBIE

COLOR ME: PART 1

IT'S ARALE FROM THE COVER ILLUSTRATION! COLOR HER IN AS YOU LIKE!

102

YES! THE ENEMY COWERS!

B-B-BLAM BANG
B-BANG
BANG BLAM

AN OUT-OF-SEASON...

BZONK

WATER-MELON CANNON!

PFFT

PHUT

EEEK!

YIPES!

GRAAAR!!

YOU'RE THE ENEMY, DR. N.

PLAYING WAR.

WHAT DO YOU THINK YOU'RE DOING!?

STOP THAT RUCKUS!

CAN'T YOU DO SOMETHING MORE... GIRL-LIKE?

LOOK, YOU TWO...

WHO DECIDED THAT!?

TOO... TOO DOO...?

ALL RIGHT, AKANE! WHAT HAVE YOU BEEN TEACHING HER...

MMM... SEN-BABY! LONG TIME NO SEE!

AAH! AAH!

BUT THEY'RE ALL NUDE.

HE'S READING THIS?

AHMAN UHHUN UHHUN EHHUH OHHUH

LECHER

IF YOU MUST ROMP, ROMP OUTSIDE.

I'M READING, OKAY!?

104

I'LL TAKE THE LENSES OUT.

WHOA!

YUP YUP!

LEMME BORROW THOSE.

UM... THAT'S THE DRESSER.

YOU'VE GOTTEN FATTER, AKANE.

NEXT, THE CLOTHES.

RIGHT!

ROGER!

OKAY, YOU'RE AKANE KIMIDORI! GO HOME!

SNAP!

TA-DAAAH!

OOOH.

BYE-BYE, DR. N!

HUH!?

DUMB TOAD ON A... NIGHT ROAD... ♪

BIG CLOWN IN A... BIG TOWN... ♪

OH, SENBEI?

WHAT DOES SHE TAKE ME FOR? I'LL KILL HER...!

SAKE

Don't leave these in people's houses!

WEIRD FAMILY...

EH!?

WHAT'S GOTTEN INTO YOU TODAY? YOU ALWAYS CALL ME "DOCTOR."

SENBEI... HUH?

HUH!?

THERE.

OIL
オイル

UM, HEY, DOCTOR?

I'M KINDA HUNGRY! HOW 'BOUT A SNACK?

108

HEY, IT'S AKANE!

HM ?

?

AKANE, POOP DOESN'T TALK.

AAH!

IT WAS THE BIG BOSS.

WAS THAT *YOU*?

POKE POKE

Y-YOU MIGHT WANT TO WATCH IT WITH THE JOKES.

HEH HEH ...

OH MY.

BANANA ?

GORILLA! GORILLA!

THUNK

I MAY NOT BE ABLE TO DO THAT...

BUT I CAN DO THIS...!

NO, I CAN'T!!

TH-THAT'S NOTHING! THE BIG BOSS CAN DO THAT!

CAN'T DO THAT, CAN YOU? HEE HEE...

HEH HEH...

...

BEHOLD THE PICK-AND-LICK!

PICK! LICK! PICK!!

SPLUCK

WH-WHERE'S THE BATHROOM? I TOTALLY FORGOT!

HEY!

BATHROOM? WHAT ARE YOU GOING TO DO THERE?

!?

WELL... NUMBER ONE... OR, ER... NUMBER TWO...

WH-WHAT...?

HAH! GOOD ONE, ARALE! YOU KNOW YOU CAN'T DO EITHER!

WHEN DO I LOOK LIKE THAT!?

NOW.

THE DOCTOR Arale Norimaki 7th Grade

DONE!

THERE!

MMPH!

WHAT ARE YOU MAKING, DOCTOR?

NAY, EPOCH-MAKING!

I'VE INVENTED SOMETHING AMAZING!

WRONG!

NEAT! A FLASH-LIGHT!

117

THE BIG-SMALL RAY GUN CAN CHANGE THE SIZE OF ANYTHING IT SHOOTS AT WILL!

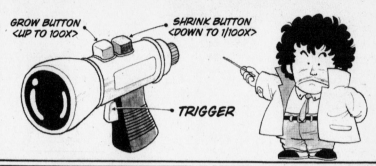

GROW BUTTON
<UP TO 100X>

SHRINK BUTTON
<DOWN TO 1/100X>

TRIGGER

GROOOW

TAKE THAT!

BZZZZ

FOR EXAMPLE...

KLIK

WELL? YOU SEE?

WOW!

BONK

SHHHRINK

FOR MY NEXT DEMONSTRATION...

KLIK

HA HA HA! AMAZING, HUH?

H-HEY!

GOT YOU NOW!

MMPH.

YOU EVEN FIT IN MY MOUTH!

GULP

119

M-MY EYE-BALL!

AAAH!

ROLL ROLL

THUNK

PLOOP

W-WATCH IT! I'M *HUMAN!* REMEMBER!?

UM, THAT'S AN ORANGE.

SPLORK

LOOK AT THAT CHART AND KNOW MY GENIUS!

OF COURSE!

IS YOUR GUN USEFUL FOR ANYTHING?

BIG-SMALL RAY GUN
EXAMPLES OF USE: A SMALL SELECTION

SAVE
ON
FAMILY
TRAIN
TRIPS!

NEVER
HAVE
TROUBLE
PACKING
LIGHT!

WH-WH-WHOA!

CITY
KIDS
CAN
PLAY
INDOORS
!

NEVER
GET
ANOTHER
PARKING
TICKET!

CONSERVE
BATH
WATER
!

MINNOW

MINI-BULB

RICE

AAA

SAVE ON
SHOPPING
EXPENSES!

I THOUGHT
IT'D TURN
INTO
$10,000!

$100

I didn't have a real one to copy!

BUT
THIS
WON'T
WORK.

POL

EFFECTIVE
AGAINST
MONSTER
ATTACKS!

122

HUH?

I THOUGHT THE DOCTOR TOOK THIS.

?

SHRINK !!

SHRINK !

IT'S A H-HAIR DRYER ...

GET THE DOOR FOR--

HEY! ARALE!

CRASH

THUDDA THUDDA...

WHA--? WH-WH-WHA--!?

OH ... OH NO.

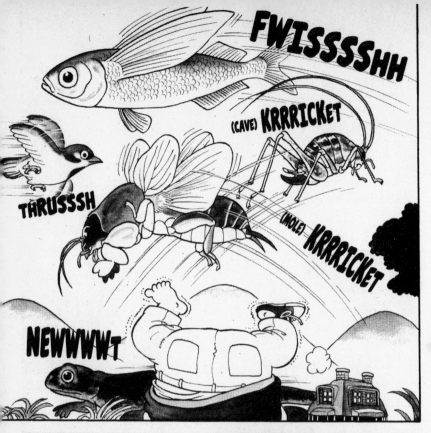

HMPH! CAN'T LEAVE YOU OUT OF MY SIGHT FOR A SECOND, CAN I!?

EH-HEH.

YOU DIDN'T ZAP ANYTHING ELSE, DID YOU!?

NOPE!

FREEBIE

FAULT FINDER

These two pictures may look the same, but there are 15 differences! Can you find them!? (I'm not telling!)

PUT PUT PUT...

SCHWAAA!!

SPRING HAS SPRUNG ON PENGUIN VILLAGE!

SLURP SLURP SLURRRP

I NEED TO FIND ME A WIFE.

POO-TEWEET PREE-TYNEAT

PREE-TYSWEET SMEL-LYFEET HEY-LET'SEAT

WHAT'S THIS, DOCTOR?

HUH?

MY "FUTURE CAMERA"! I THOUGHT I HID THIS...

OH, HEY!

WHAT'S IT DO?

YOU'VE FOUND SOMETHING VERY DANGEROUS.

?

☆ FUTURE CAMERA ☆

YEAR-SETTING DIAL

SHUTTER

YEAR METER (SHOWN SET TO "25 YEARS")

025

2005

PHOTO PRINTER

IT CAN PHOTOGRAPH THE FUTURE!

LOTS OF THINGS! FOR ONE ...

ACTUALLY, THAT'S ALL IT DOES.

ARE YOUR EARS ON RIGHT?

NOT "SUTURE," "FUTURE"!

A SUTURE CAMERA!? THAT IS DANGEROUS!

NOW, I SET THIS TO ONE YEAR...

KLIK KLIK

SEE THIS DRAGON-FLY LARVA?

PLUBBB

SNNNAP

HO-YO!

SEE?

1981

SO ARE YOU!

THAT'S A *MANGA* CHARACTER!

YOU'RE JUST LIKE DORAE-MON*!

*A ROBOTIC CAT THAT PULLS INVENTIONS FROM HIS POCKET.

HEH. BRAINS *AND* BEAUTY, KID.

YOU'RE REALLY SMART, DOCTOR!

YOU CAN SET THE DIAL TO AS MANY YEARS AS YOU WANT.

KLIK KLIK

AAAH! NO!

I'LL TAKE YOUR PICTURE!

HUH !?

SNNNAP

I-I TOLD YOU IT WAS DANGEROUS!!

BWA HA HA HA!

1995

134

SNNNNAP

HERE GOES!

HEY!

1981

PLUBBB

SEE!?

WOW, IT WORKS!

WHOA! COOL!!

I WANNA SEE! I WANNA SEE!

OKAY!

Has absolutely no concept of time.

LET'S TRY TEN YEARS.

TAKE A SHOT OF ME!

Y-YO, AKANE!

WHOA...

KLIK KLIK

SNNNAP

1990

WE'RE DOOMED.

HEY, I'M A COP!

WHOA, LOOK! I'M SO COOL!!

COOL!

1990

YOU BETTER MAKE SURE I LOOK BEAUTIFUL!

HOW DO I DO THAT...?

SURE.

TAKE ONE OF ME, ARALE.

LOOK AT YOUR BOOBS! BOING BOING!

NOT BAD!

YIPES... BOSSY AS EVER!

1990

SNNNAP

C'MON C'MON...

I WONDER WHAT YOU'LL LOOK LIKE, ARALE!

BWA HA HA HA

THIS IS TOO CRUEL...

SNNNAP

I PICTURE...

YEAH! THAT'S HER, THAT'S HER!

YOU LOOK EXACTLY THE SAME!

1990

HUH?

PLUBBB

137

138

N'cha! ☆ **Always youthful! That's Grandma Arale!** ☆

Dr SCRAP

2040: Barely Making It Through Today!

① Grandpa Senbei (88 yrs. old) ② Grandma Arale (73 yrs. old!?)
③ Grandpa Taro (75 yrs. old) ④ Grandpa Peasuke (73 yrs. old)
⑤ Grandma Akane (73 yrs. old)

Pen-dragging, doddering

Akira Toriyama

141

The Time Slipper

TWEET
TWEET

DAWN HAS DAWNED ON *PENGUIN VILLAGE!*

AH...A RELAXING SUNDAY MORN'.

SUNDAY? WHAT'S SUNDAY?

YAWN.

FINISHED AT LAST!

WHEW. WHERE'S ARALE?

IT'S MORNING ALREADY ...

144

WH-WHAT!?

ZZZZ ZZZZ

URK!?

R-ROBOTS **DON'T** SNORE! OR **SLEEP!!**

DON'T YOU "N'CHA." ME!!

N'CHA.

...

VWOOSH VWOOSH

HOW COME YOU ONLY MIMIC THE DUMB HUMAN STUFF!?

MAN ...

SOAP

↳ SHE'S WASHING HER FACE, NOT DOING THE LAUNDRY.

I'VE INVENTED SOMETHING TRULY AMAZING.

ARALE!

WHAT DID YOU MAKE, DOCTOR?

FIRST PANTS, *THEN* QUESTIONS!

TIME *SLIPPER*!

TIME SLEEPER?

THE TIME SLIPPER!!

NO, NO, NO! TIME *SLIPPER!*

TIME STRIPPER?

BRRR

A MACHINE THAT USES A TIME SLIP* TO TRAVEL FREELY THROUGH TIME!

*TIME SLIPS OCCUR WHEN A JOLT TO THE SPACE-TIME CONTINUUM CAUSES THINGS TO APPEAR IN ANOTHER TIME.

147

THE TIME SLIPPER: AN EASY GUIDE

⟨ MR. TIME ⟩

★ THE TIME SLIPPER HAS TWO PARTS: "MR. TIME" AND "SLIPPERY BOARD."

SELECTOR (PUSH FOR PAST, PULL FOR FUTURE)

YEAR DIAL

YEAR METER

BACK VIEW

CORD ATTACHMENT

SWITCH

MR. TIME

CORD

SLIPPERY BOARD

TO GO, SAY, 500 YEARS IN THE PAST, WE SET THE DIAL TO 5-0-0.

DRRRR DRRRR

FIRST, WE TURN MR. TIME'S SWITCH TO "ON."

THEN, WE PLACE IT ON THE SLIPPERY BOARD AND...

PRESS DOWN THE SELECTOR TO GO BACK IN TIME!

KLUNK

AHEM...THANK YOU FOR CHOOSING TIME SLIP!

KRIK

A-YA?

BWEEEE

AH!

THAT'S FOR LICKING! NOT HITTING!

DONK DONK

A LOLLIPOP, AS A TOKEN OF OUR GRATITUDE.

I'M MR. TIME. I'LL BE YOUR GUIDE TODAY!

HERE!

LET'S BEGIN OUR JOURNEY THROUGH TIME!

WITHOUT FURTHER ADO...

HERE WE GO!

READY?

GET ON WITH IT ALREADY!

THIS WASN'T IN MY PROGRAM...

PUFF PUFF

PACE PACE

WHAT HAVE I DONE!?

WHAT CAN I DO?

WHAT DO I DO?

INDIFFERENT, THE SUN SET...

SEE YA TOMORROW!

SPLASH

OR SO HE TOLD HIMSELF...

MR. TIME'S STILL WITH HER!

W-WELL...

THEY'LL BE BACK IN NO TIME! HA!

REAL BAD!!

THIS IS BAD.

155

*JAPAN'S RIP VAN WINKLE

FREEBIE

COLOR ME: PART 2

ARALE

The Mysterious Egg

HELLO BOYS AND GIRLS! GOOD MORNOONING!* IN THIS EPISODE, THE DOCTOR USES HIS TIME SLIPPER TO TAKE US TO THE PREHISTORIC PAST!

*A MISHMASH OF "GOOD MORNING," "...AFTERNOON" AND "...EVENING." PRETTY DUMB, HUH?

YOU'RE REALLY GOING TO WEAR THAT?

WHERE IS EVERY-ONE?

SORRY I'M LATE!

N'CHA!

HEY! PEASUKE MADE IT!

158

I MADE IT MYSELF!

HA HA. NICE COSTUME, ARALE!

TH-THIS ISN'T SOME KIND OF SCHOOL TRIP...

I DUNNO.

AKANE?

OH, SORRY. HE'S AT A BALLGAME.

WHERE'S TARO?

SORRY... MY HEAD REALLY HURTS.

UH... DR. N?

THAT IDIOT...

DRRR DRRR

MY GREATEST INVENTION EVER, AND THEY DON'T CARE!!

GRRR... WHAT'S WITH THESE PEOPLE!?

159

CHOMP CHOMP

WHAT'S THE NET FOR?

THIS?

I'M GOING TO CATCH A DINOSAUR!

SEE IF I EVER LET ANY OF THEM RIDE!

FINE! IT'LL BE JUST US THREE!

?

N-NO WAY!

WHAT!? THEY'RE THAT BIG!?

GUIDE TO THE DINOSAURS

WHOA! WOW! WHOO!

WILL WE LIVE TO SEE TOMOR-ROW?

HOW COULD I NOT KNOW THAT!?

IT WAS A JOKE! A JOKE!

EH HEH HEH... I-I KNEW THAT!

GUIDE TO THE DINOSAURS

NUMB-RAY GUN

160

YAY, YAY!

GO, GO, GO!!

OKAY! I THINK IT'S TIME!

HUH? WHAT?

WE'RE IN JUNIOR HIGH!

POOOO!

I FELT LIKE A PRE-SCHOOL TEACHER.

N-NOTHING. JUST, FOR A SECOND THERE...

KLUNK

YEAH, YEAH, LET'S GO ALREADY!

UM... WE'RE IN LUCK WITH CLEAR SKIES TODAY...!

HIYA, HIYA!

AH!

*A BOWL OF RICE AND BEEF

HUH?

WHAT'S THIS?

SKRITCH SKRITCH

WOW. YOU SURE KNOW A LOT.

WAAAARGH

HRUK

OH, RIGHT!

GRRRRR!!

WAAAH! WADDLE WE DO!? WADDLE WE DO!?

DR. N! RAY GUN! RAY GUN!

WAH HA HA! YOU HAVEN'T EVOLVED ONE BIT!!

HE'S YOUR SPITTING IMAGE! MUST BE YOUR ANCESTOR!

HO-YO-YO...

DOCTOR, DOCTOR!

BWA HA HA HA HA HA HA

...

AH!

SLUMP

HE'S MAKING A FIRE!

MMPH.

MMPH.

WHAT'RE YOU DOING?

HUH?

ZUK ZUK

CHEER UP!

C'MON, I'M SORRY!

YOU WENT TOO FAR, DR. N!

PRESENT-DAY! PRESENT-DAY! THANKS FOR RIDING!

YOU LOOK LIKE A TANUKI*!

HERE! HERE!

HEY, ARALE? WHERE'S YOUR EGG?

*A BIG-BELLIED RACCOON-DOG. (SEE PANEL 3, PAGE 108.)

THOSE ARE MOVIE MONSTERS ...

WHAT DO WE DO IF IT HATCHES ONE OF THESE?

UM, HEY ...

GODZILLA   MOTHRA

SENBEI & ARALE NORIMAKI

170

MAYBE IT'S A TYRANNO-SAURUS! OR A TRICERA-TOPS!

WH-WHOA! IT'S HATCHING!

YAY YAY!

KRRAK KRRRACK

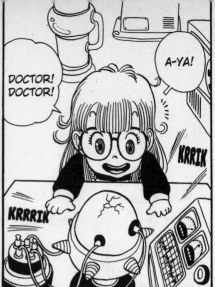

DOCTOR! DOCTOR!

A-YA!

KRRIK

KRRRIK

POP

PLIK KRRAK KRRRACK

KRRAK KRIK KRRAK

HO-YO-YO-YO!

ER...A S-STEGO-SAUR.. MAYBE?

UM, PEASUKE ...?

Look! A signed
Toriyama! Hang
it on your wall!

Is It a Girl!?
Is It a Boy!?

174

THAT'S MY BIGGEST FEAR...

ARALE WOULD GET MAD, AND THERE'S NO TELLING WHAT SHE'D DO.

I CAN'T TAKE IT BACK TO THE PAST ...

WHAT TO DO WITH THIS KID!?

KOO POO POO!

LOOK!

D-DON'T TEACH IT THAT!!

Y-YOU *CAN'T* NURSE!

WANT TO NURSE?

REAL KIDS *CAN'T* NURSE!

BUT YOU SAID I WAS THE PERFECT HUMAN REPLICA!

MEN DON'T NURSE. IT'D BE JUST... GROSS, OKAY!?

OKAY, YOU NURSE IT!

E-ER... SHE SAID, "IDIOT! DUMMY! DIE, PERVERT!" R-RATHER LOUDLY...

WELL? WHAT DID SHE SAY?

"AOI? I NEED YOUR BOOBS!"

HANG ON, I'LL ASK AOI.

DRRR DRRR

? ? ?

SUCH MODERN CONVEN- IENCES!

HM ...

178

WHY DO I HAVE A BABY!? UNNHHH...

I'M NOT MARRIED... I-I HAVEN'T EVEN HELD HANDS!

SOB SOB

SLUMP

SLURP SLURP

YOU DRINK JUST LIKE ME!

HEH HEH...

IT EATS ANYTHING!

CRUNCH CRUNCH

WHAT!?

DOCTOR! DOCTOR!

SLUMP

SLUMP

AWAH WAH WAAAH!

BROOM.

SNARF SNARF...

GAAAAAH!!

NOW, DON'T EAT ME!

I-IT WAS BAD ENOUGH THAT IT CAME OUT OF AN EGG...AND FULLY CLOTHED!

MUNCH MUNCH

WH-WHAT KIND OF BABY IS THAT!?

CAN IT SHARPEN PENCILS?

SNARF SNARF

I GUESS IT *COULD* BE USEFUL...

WON'T NEED A TRASH-CAN...

W-WELL...

HOO HOO

WHOO! UP HIGH, UP HIGH YOU GO!

DIMWHIT DIMWHIT

HEH...

HM... NICE TRY.

180

UP HIGH, UP HIGH!!

KRACK

DON'T DROP IT, OKAY?

I WANT TO TRY!

TOO HIGH!!

HO-YO! HIGH, HIGH!

HYAA-ARGH!

IT FELL.

SHE HAS ABSO-LUTELY NO CONTROL!

WH-WHAT KIND OF BABY...

I GIVE UP.

HOO HOO

WHUMP

YUP!

HUH? YOU TAKING A BATH, TOO?

I GOTTA GIVE YOU A BATH!

YEEARGH! YOU'RE ALL DIRTY!

H-HEY! GIMME SPACE, OKAY? IT'S EMBARRASSING!

N-NO PEEKING.

?

FLIT FLIT FLIT

I'LL TRY NOT TO THINK TOO HARD ABOUT THIS ONE.

KUH-WOOOL!

HO-YO-YO-YO!!

TH-THIS BABY'S GOT WINGS...!

FLIT

GNAW GNAW GNAW

NO EATING THE BATH!

...OR NOT!

HEYA! Y'KNOW, IT MIGHT JUST BE ONE OF THEM *ANGELS*!

?

NOT EVEN...

NOTHING THERE!

HEY! IT'S THE SAME AS ME!

...THAT.

HUH?

IS IT BOY? IS IT A GIRL?

SHE THINKS GIRLS HAVE NOTHING DOWN THERE.

HEH! R-RIGHT! EH... EH-HEH!

IT'S A GIRL!

HOO HOO. I SEE.

NIGHTFALL HAS FALLEN ON PENGUIN VILLAGE!!

PEEE!

OKAY! LIL' GODZILLA!

WE SHOULD GIVE HER A NAME.

HMM ... RIGHT.

NOT *THAT* NAME!

NO MONSTERS!

"GAMERA," THEN!

TWO WORDS: ATOMIC RAYS!!

WHY?

F-FINE! FINE! CALL HER WHATEVER!

MY HEAD HURTS.

PANT

PANT

PANT

CAT!

WHISKERS?

THAT'S A DOG!

UM... POOCH!

MANGA!

JUMP?

RIBBIT?

SEN-BEI?

THAT'S ME!

FROG!

184

END OF VOLUME 1

In The Next Volume

A bumbling alien arrives on Earth in hopes of becoming the savior of the planet, but he doesn't count on Arale upstaging his efforts at every turn! The cute little android also outwits a gun-toting bank robber who kidnaps her and her friend Gatchan, and, naturally, he lives to regret it... And Arale's dream of flying finally comes true! All this and more in volume 2 of **Dr. Slump**!

Available in July 2005!